# CHILDREN
## *Stories*

Anita Srivastava

Archway Publishing books may be ordered through booksellers or by contacting:

Archway Publishing
1663 Liberty Drive
Bloomington, IN 47403
www.archwaypublishing.com
844-669-3957

Because of the dynamic nature of the Internet, any web addresses or links contained
in this book may have changed since publication and may no longer be valid. The views
expressed in this work are solely those of the author and do not necessarily reflect the views
of the publisher, and the publisher hereby disclaims any responsibility for them.

ISBN: 978-1-6657-2333-6 (sc)
ISBN: 978-1-6657-2334-3 (hc)
ISBN: 978-1-6657-2332-9 (e)

Print information available on the last page.

Archway Publishing rev. date: 05/10/2022

# Contents

# A Beautiful Friendship

It was a nice summer morning. After five days of cloudy days and constant rain, the sun was finally out. There was a cool breeze and one could see a ray of sunshine peeking through the trees. Everything looked washed and new. Sophia was very happy because it was the first day she could go out and play in the park. She was looking forward to going out as soon as she got dressed. She was curious to meet kids in the neighbourhood and make new friends.

Her family had moved to Lalendorf only a month ago. It was a relatively smaller town than Berlin where they lived until they came here. Her grandparents who lived here, owned a small farm and a house and they wanted her father to move back as they were getting too old to manage on their own. Her parents also looked at it as good opportunity for Sophia to get to know her grandparents as well as grow up in a small and safe town. Now Sophia was not so sure as she had to leave all her childhood friends behind and also she did not know how she would like living in a smaller town. Therefore, today was a good day for her to explore and find out for herself. School was opening in few weeks time. Her parents had taken her to the new school to meet her teacher so she would not feel afraid on her first day. School building was small but nice. There were many classrooms. In the back of the school was a playground with many fruit trees surrounding the school boundary. In one corner there was a beautiful garden with many flowers and pretty bushes whose names she did not know. She liked her school and found her teacher to be a nice middle aged lady. Teacher showed her all the books she kept in her library which were available for students to borrow. Sophia was a reader and she could not wait for school to begin so she could borrow books.

On this beautiful day, Sophia wanted to go outside, but her mother called her for breakfast and told her to help her with a party for grandma as today was her birthday. Sophia knew better not to argue with her mom but she did not like the idea of staying home and not enjoy playing outside. They both agreed that she would go out for few hours and play in the park and come back to help mom bake the cake. Sophia decided to ride her bike to the park which was only five minutes away from her house. It was a small park with some rides and swing sets and a playground to play football. There were just few children playing there. She introduced herself to them and told them she was new to the town and would like to make new friends. Soon she

found out that the town had very few children and most of them were older than her. There was one girl who was closer to her age and she was in 6<sup>th</sup> grade, a grade higher than Sophia. Her name was Mika and Mika told her that the school was small but it was a nice and friendly place. Sophia's teacher was a nice lady but very strict in classroom. She did not like her students to be noisy but she never punished them. School work was easy and there was not much homework.

Sophia was having fun but it was time to go home as she had promised her mother she would help. Also grandparents were coming around lunch time. She was on her way to home when she noticed a herd of tall animals running very fast on the other side of the fence. She noticed one of them smaller than others, was moving very slow and looking at Sophia with curiosity. Sophia stopped to look at them but became fearful of them. She had never seen these animals before. They were slender and looked little bit like deer but Sophia did not know if they were dangerous. She quickly got inside the safe confinement of her kitchen. Mother was busy preparing midday food. She asked her daughter what was the matter as she looked scared. Sophia explained that she saw some strange, very tall animals and she did not know what were they called. Mom looked through the kitchen window and saw the group of animals running. She told her daughter they were Antelope and mostly curious but harmless animals but Sophia was not convinced.

Sophia started noticing that the smaller Antelope would come close to her fence and constantly look towards the house. One day she gathered her courage and came out to look at the animal. From that day onwards, she would come out and go closer to the fence and one day she went so close to the animal that she could reach out and touch it. Soon she realised that the animal just wanted to be close to her and be playful. Sophia's mom also found out that the Antelope was an orphan whose mother was killed in a road accident. A couple brought Antelope to their home and cared for it till the baby grew old enough to survive on its own. Antelope enjoyed human company and always hung around homes. Knowing this, Sophia changed her attitude towards the animal and started bringing two apples, one for herself and another for the animal. Soon it became a game for both of them to have an apple and spend some time together. Sophia was enjoying their time together and decided to give the Antelope a name. She chose the name Harira and whenever she called Harira, it came running to her. It became her routine to see Harira before she went to school and she found Harira waiting for her everyday by the fence when she came back from school. They both seemed to enjoy each other's company and the fruit they shared together. On weekends both played game of running on either side of fence but Harira was so fast that it beat Sophia every time. Both were happy in each other's company and parents were happy to see Sophia getting to like her new environment.

One Saturday morning, Sophia thought about exploring the town. She had not gone beyond the park and today she decided to see for herself what was beyond the boundary of the park and the school. She asked her mother and mother thought for a moment and decided it was safe in the town for her go out for few hours. Sophia was very happy and she quickly finished her breakfast of schnitzel and brotchen and kissed mother goodbye. She got on her bike and rode towards the park. She looked around and saw the park was empty so she kept going. She saw rows of homes, open fields and some farm lands. There were some cows grazing and heron and goose playing by the little lake.

There were fruit trees all around and it was a very pretty sight. She noticed a small rabbit hopping happily in the field trying to find something to eat.

Soon Sophia felt very tired and decided to take a break before returning home. She sat down on the grass and after few minutes got on her bike to go home. Sophia realized that she had no idea which way was home. She was very puzzled and little scared. Realizing that she did not know how to get home, she panicked and started crying. She was not only scared but was also getting hungry. There was not a single person on the road except the animals and birds and they could not help her. She went in one direction, but found it unfamiliar. Very upset with herself and not knowing what to do she shouted for help hoping someone might hear her. Nothing! She sat down in desperation and suddenly she felt someone nudging her in the back. She turned around and what did she find? It was none other than her friend Harira. She had never felt so happy to see anyone as she was to see her friend at that moment. She did not know that Harira was always following her when she started on her expedition and keeping an watchful eye on her. She hugged and kissed him. Harira pointed in the right direction and both of them reached home in no time. When Sophia reached home. She was too excited to tell her mother the whole story of her adventurous morning. Mother was very happy and both of them came out to thank Harira. He was standing proud and he earned lots of hugs and then both Sophia and Harira shared their apple together. From that day onwards, Harira was allowed to come inside the fence and Sophia played with her best friend everyday.

"Don't walk behind me; I may not lead. Don't walk in front of me; I may not follow. Just walk beside me and be my friend." By Albert Camus

# My Ohana

Last we heard of Darsh, he was growing up very nicely in friendly and warm waters of Indian Ocean. Darsh, a very social and outgoing dolphin, liked playing with other dolphins and fish in the water. He was almost two year old and his parents were still very protective of him from any danger but Darsh had strong desire to explore new things and surroundings. He was getting very bored with the sameness of everything and the wanderlust in him was telling him to travel to new places but he was concerned about leaving his parents and even telling them what was going through his head. One day he gathered enough courage to sit down with mom and talk to her. He knew mom was more receptive to new ideas and would be willing to at least listen. He told mom that he wanted to go see the world and explore new territories. Mother did not say anything except that she would talk to his father and then they will talk at a later day. Darsh was encouraged that his mother's first reaction was not to get angry.

After few day, Darsh's parents asked him to come for a family meeting to discuss his desire to explore new territories. They had many questions but Darsh was prepared. He was able to answer all their questions. He told them he had already thought about many details and he had a friend who wanted to go with him as well. He knew that the journey was long and tiring but he had already figured out the path. He explained to them that he had mapped out his trip by swimming eastward through Polynesian islands to Pacific Ocean. Since the water in different parts would be cold, they would start when it was hot in summer and once they reached Hawaii, the water would be nice and warm. After an hour of talking, parent told him that he should go and explore the world. Darsh could not hide his excitement and he swam quickly to tell his friend that the mission was a go and they should leave within a week. Two started planning their trip carefully. They figured out that they will have to travel very far and also through different environment, different population of people and fish in water. Next week came soon enough. Both of them said good bye to their parents and friends and swam off to the far off land.

They had seen many trade ships taking similar route carrying many export items and Darsh decided to follow these ships. Two of them swam for most of the day and rested in the night time. Weeks passed and both decided to spend few days in the country they had arrived last evening. They found everything was different here. There were really very tall people swimming in the ocean also they were speaking in a tongue that they heard rarely in their home country. The fish in water were very colorful and very large. They started enjoying their new environment making new friends but soon realized that they must make a move if they were to get to Hawaii before the water got very cold. It took them many weeks of swimming before they realized they were in new territory.

Darsh heard someone say " Aloha". What does aloha mean, he had no idea. He looked up to see a dolphin or nai'a talking to him. Darsh said hello and asked him what was the name of the place. Dolphin said he was in waters of Hawaii and he was much welcome. Darsh liked his new friend immediately and knew that he was going to like this place. The water was warm, plentiful of fish of all sizes and colors and mostly he saw many large fish called Salmon which he had never seen before and nai'a. He started to get settled by exploring new territories and friends. He soon found out that he was accepted by the Kama'ainas(natives) and became part of a large Ohana(family). Darsh liked this concept of Ohana very much and he loved not feeling an outsider. He would notice many people surf riding or swimming and playing in the warm water. Some of them spoke language that Darsh had heard before but some also spoke pidgin, a local language.

One day he noticed a little girl standing on the shore and looking very sad. Darsh asked her why she was sad. The girl told him that she would like to go in water but she was afraid as she did not know how to swim. Darsh thought for a moment and told the girl that she could sit on his back and he would take her for short ride. The girl liked the idea and did the same. While swimming, two of them started talking. The girl asked him what was he called. Darsh told her his name and told her that he had swam all the way from Indian Ocean and saw different countries and different people. He told her he liked it here very much because water is always warm, the flowers were pretty and most of all he liked people and the polite language everyone spoke. He told her he has even seen beautiful girls with flowers in their hair, dancing the hula dance. Girl told him her name is Kalani which means joy and she comes here often with her tutu (grandmother) and would like to see him again. She really enjoyed swimming with him because she was not afraid. At that time her tutu came and was surprised to see her with a dolphin. kalani told tutu that she made a new friend and she enjoyed her time with him. Tutu was happy but told her it was time to go. They said goodbye. When Darsh's friend saw everything from a distance he asked him who was the keiki (child) he was swimming with. Darsh told him her name is Kalani and she is his new friend. Kalani would tell Darsh about her life on the island and Darsh would tell all about his life in east and his travel to Australia and people there. They enjoyed their talk a lot. One day Kalani told Darsh that he had Aloha spirit which means love and compassion. She explained that in Hawaii people were always happy and considered everyone like family or Ohana. Darsh liked the concept of Ohana because he had never experienced this anywhere else in his short life.

Kalani would come to the beach every few days and Darsh and she spent many hours playing in the water or swimming or just talking. Kalani told him she was in school half day and then she spent time with tutu. She told all her friends at school about her new friend but they did not believe her so she had asked tutu to take a picture of both of them in the water. Darsh would tell her stories of his life in Indian Ocean and his parents and he missed it sometimes. But life was good with his Ohana and he looked forward to his time with Kalani. In few weeks, Kalani stopped being afraid of water and she started to swim in the shallow water. Darsh would always watch over her and tutu also felt good about leaving Kalani for short time to visit her friends on the beach.

One day early morning, Darsh noticed lots of commotion on the beach. There were lots of family and friends were on the beach wearing beautiful yellow lei made out of ilima flowers and having lots of fun. Some people were cooking breakfast, food of sausage or eggs and some were trying to pitch tent as cover from sun. Kids were playing different games of hula hoops race or Leis hide and seek. Darsh was curious to know what was going on. He went to his friend from the ocean but couldn't find him. Then he noticed Kalani was with large group of people and having fun. He swam close to her and asked her what was special about this day. She explained that today was Leis day and everyone celebrated the day by exchanging Leis with family and friends. Every island in Hawaii has different color and flower Leis and the day signifies love and hope for everyone.

One day when Kalani came to the beach and did not see her friend, she decided to go in the water on her own. Suddenly, there was a big wave that pushed Kalani little more deeper for her comfort. Kalani felt very scared especially since Darsh was not around and she started crying. Darsh was not far and he was surprised to hear a cry for help coming from the water. He quickly saw that Kalani was in trouble. Darsh got in to action and swam alongside Kalani and brought her safely to the shore and on the beach. He consoled her and told her that she was safe and had no reason to cry anymore. Tutu came running too to see what was going on. Both friends kept quiet as they didn't want her to worry and resumed their play as if nothing was wrong.

Kalani and Darsh became best friends. Sometimes Kalani would bring fish for him and Darsh would take her for ride on his back. Kalani stopped being afraid of water and slowly she started going in water away from shore although she was always careful to stay close to the beach if she feared water to be very active with big tides. Darsh also hung around her if the waves were high. Sometimes Kalani would bring her friends with her and all of them played many games and took turns to swim with Darsh. Darsh's friends were happy to see him enjoying and they knew that he would stay with them for long time. Darsh also decided that he would stay in these water and make it his home. He knew he would always miss his parents but he knew that he was home away from home.

"I feel at ease and, in an indefinable way, at home, when dolphins are around. I now know they are nearby before they appear. I dream after they leave." By Virginia Coyle

# Magic feather

It was a beautiful spring morning. The sun was shining, temperature was neither cold nor too warm. The birds were beginning to come back from their hibernation. The trees were starting to have new leaves, nice and green and beautiful. Very soon, new buds will start appearing and trees and bushes will be full of pretty and colourful flowers. Maliya was hopping in her front yard. She was slightly bored and looking to do something fun. Maliya was eight years old and in third grade. She did have few friends but not too many. She had a older brother, Aaron who was eleven years old and in sixth grade. Aaron was a quite boy and very well behaved all the time. His grades at school were very good. He was respectful to all adults and everyone liked him.

Now Maliya was a different story. She was very mischievous and got into trouble a lot at school and at home. She just wanted to have fun and she never thought about consequences of her actions. She did not pay much attention to her studies and her grades were not very good. One day, she was walking home after her school, she noticed a very tiny feather on the ground. The beautiful, colorfull feather caught her attention and she stopped to pick it up. There was an old Indian man standing nearby and he told her that it was a magic feather and she must keep it very safely and never lose it. He said whoever has the feather will always have good luck.

Maliya quickly ran home and went straight to her room. She put the feather in a small box and kept the box in her school bag. She wanted to do well in her studies just like Aaron so her parents would be proud of her too. That night she went to bed very happy. Next day, at school she was very attentive to her teacher and tried not to get in trouble. She started paying attention to her school work and her lessons. She thought to herself, it must be the magic feather. Soon her grades started to improve and she was not getting into much trouble at home and at school. She made sure that she always had the little box with the tiny feather in it with her.

End of the school year was coming closer and soon it would be summer holidays. Maliya was supposed to visit her grandma in another city for most of the summer. She liked swimming in

the pool and playing in the backyard a lot at grandma's home. But end of the year also meant big tests that everyone had to take to move to next grade. Maliya was not too fond of these tests but this time she was not afraid because she knew she had the magic feather and she was confident she would do well. The day of the test, she went to her classroom and looked in her bag to get the box out. She wanted to have the feather in front of her to be sure of good luck. But she was shocked to find that the box was not in the school bag. Oh my goodness! What am I supposed to do now. But there was no time. She completed the whole test but she was rather nervous whole time.

The report card was supposed to come in one week time. One day the report card came in the mail. Without opening it she gave it her mother and ran to her room. She was afraid to even stay in the same room. Soon, she heard her mom calling her. She went to her very quietly because she knew her grades were not good because she had lost her good luck feather. She saw her mother smiling, she was puzzled. She snatched the report card from her hand and saw she had gotten mostly As, there was only one B in spelling. Maliya could not believe it. She told her mom the whole story of good luck magic feather and how she had lost it. So she was afraid that she lost her good luck too. Mom smiled and said " magic is not in the feather but believing in its magic". She explained that ever since Maliya found the feather, she started believing what the Indian man had told her. But really it was Maliya who started believing in herself but told herself it was the feather that made her do better in school. The whole truth is that if you have faith that you will do better, then you will do better. So even though Maliya had misplaced her box of feather, she still did well in the tests. She was always capable but she did not know it.

Maliya gave a big hug to her mom and ran to her room humming a song. She started to put her school bag in her closet and what does she find, she finds her tiny box lying on the floor. She was very happy to find it but she knew that from now onwards, she needed no good luck feather because she knew the secret of doing well in school and at home. She was her own good luck

"A feather is a sign from the angels. It is a response to a question, a thought or an emotion. It is their way of saying you are being loved and are guided through this by the angelic realm" Eileen Anglin

# Meena Was Up Early

Meena was up early. It was still dark and the sun would not be out for next hour or so. She had lots to do before she would go to school. It was not really a proper school with many classroom and teachers as well as students. But it was a lady who lived close to her home, taught her at her home. Meena was lucky to have met her one day at the local grocer. As Meena was struggling with calculating the price of her purchase, this nice lady who was behinds her in the line quickly helped her out with the calculation. As both left the store, they started talking. Meena found out that the lady was called Mrs Sinha and she had just moved from a nearby town. She was semi-retired teacher and was looking to do something with her time. Mrs Sinha asked Meena why she was not in school to which she replied that she was not allowed to. Mrs Sinha was surprised to hear this and told Meena to come to her home if she ever had time as she would like to talk to her.

One day, Meena decided that she would go visit this nice lady. She asked permission from her mom and went to see the lady in the afternoon. Mrs Sinha was sitting in her small garden and reading a book. She was surprised but happy to see Meena. She asked her to sit down and offered her a cup of tea. They started talking and Mrs Sinha told Meena that she had recently moved to her childhood home after the death of her husband. Previously, She lived in big city and ran school for girls. Her son is married and lives far off but her daughter is finishing up her degree in nearby city. Meena told her that going to school was a struggle for her as she had to fight with her parents to let her attend local school. She was the eldest of four children her parents had but she was the only girl. It was a unspoken understanding in the family that girls never went to school and they mostly learnt from the boys. Most of the girls in the neighbourhood stayed home and learnt to do housework and took care of everybody. Although many girls in Meena's neighbourhood stayed home, Meena was not happy with her situation as she found house work tiresome and boring. She tried to go to school many times in the morning but her father always blocked her way. Meena tried to argue that if she went to school, she would learn to read and do simple calculations especially when she went to market with her mom to buy vegetables. Parents argued that her brothers had to be educated to get

jobs to help out the family but Meena would be married when she was old enough, may be at age 16 and then she would have to do the same at her in-laws home. Mrs Sinha was surprised to hear this. She asked her if she liked going to school to which Meena replied that she wished she could go back to school and learn. Mrs Sinha asked her to come back to her house same time in few days.

Meena got home in time to start the evening meal but she enjoyed her time with Mrs Sinha a lot. She was very curious and she could not wait and went to see her in two days. When she arrived there, she found a small desk and chair. There was notebook and few books and writing pen and pencil. She was confused and picked up the notebook. Top of the first page, her name was written. Underneath was a short quote " if you educate a girl, you educate the whole nation". Seeing a confused look on Meena's face, Mrs Sinha or auntie as she was called told her that it was a shame that such a smart and willing student had to stop learning. She told Meena that from this day onward she will be taught here at home provided she was willing to work hard. If Meena can not go to school, auntie will bring the school to her. Hearing this Meena jumped with joy. Suddenly she remembered that her mother may object to this arrangement. Auntie told her not to worry and she will take care of everything.

Meena started learning and she even found time to do her homework. Meena went to autie's home everyday after the morning chore and stayed there for two hours learning all the subjects. Meena found out that she liked learning about history especially when auntie taught her about the history of education of women in the world. She liked auntie talk about women of Vedic time who enjoyed freedom of gender equality and were equally educated as men. But all of this was lost during British period. She could not understand why girls were prohibited from going to school. She decided that there was nothing that will stop her from learning. She stared reading about history of women's education especially about the first girls school opened by Savitribai Phule in 19th century. She was a reformer and women's right advocate. More she read about the history of women's right, she decided that there was nothing that will stop her in her persuit of self improvement in the field of education.

Meena started going to auntie's home everyday and worked very hard at home to complete her homework. She started bringing books from auntie and read them in the evening. Auntie told her that she was a very bright student and she would be ready to take her high school examination in a very short time. This encouraged Meena very much and she decided to take her exams in few months. Soon it was time and Meena went to the centre with auntie and wrote her final exams. Meena spent next month or so in lots of anxiety and worries but the day could not come soon enough. She was afraid go look and had her brother look for her name in the paper. Her brother wanted to see her reaction and so told her her name was not in the paper. Meena was almost on the verge of crying when her brother told her that he was only teasing her and she actually passed with flying colours and her name was in top ranking. Meena could not believe that and the whole household erupted in a big cheer and happiness. Family decided to have a big party and Auntie was invited to their home to join them in the celebration. Auntie was praised a lot for all she did for Meena but she wouldn't hear none of this. She told the family that Meena was very bright and she must join a proper college and get her degree.

Few days later, father called Meena and said he wanted to talk to her. It was first time father talked to her about her interest in school and what she wanted to do in future. Meena told him about her interest in finishing her college degree and get a job teaching mostly girls. But what about marriage, her father asked. Meena said she has not thought about it and she definitely wants to have experience of learning. It was decided that Meena will go and apply for college admission. Meena could not contain her excitement and she ran to tell auntie about this. Auntie was overjoyed and they both set a time for next day to go to nearby college. Meena not only got admission to the college but also got scholarship based on her excellence in high school exams. This was turning out to a very good day for both of them. Auntie decided to stop at a small cafe and celebrate this day with Meena. Auntie also had a plan that she wanted to discuss with Meena. She wanted to open a school for girls like Meena who could not go to regular school and teach them. Meena loved the idea and told her that she would help her anyway she could. Auntie told her to find the students and help her organize lessons. From that day onward, two of them got busy with getting ready to open school. Meena found students and brought them to auntie's home. Meena also used her free time to teach. Meena could not help recalling the quote in her notebook that auntie had prepared for her "educate a girl, you educate the whole nation". Student of yesterday became teacher of present.

"The skill of a teacher to a worthy student attains greater excellence as the water of a cloud is turned into a pearl in a sea shell" by Unknown teacher.

# Story of Baby Pigeon

It was a nice town. Beautiful trees, pretty flowers. Nice blue sky and beautiful beaches. The ocean water was blue and there was trade wind blowing most days which made the weather always nice. Birds were flying and singing happy songs. As usual Myna was perched on the Lanai railing and singing. she knew only one song and she knew that the couple who lived there liked to hear her sing and they rewarded her with human food. Myna liked the food very much because it was soft to bite and had nice flavor and taste. Sometimes she brought her companion because she knew there will always be food for them. It was a nice couple who lived there. Not too old, not too young but kind and simple people and most of all they enjoyed watching birds.

Now pigeons were also friendly and always exploring new places to visit. It was a beautiful spring morning and one female pigeon started her day in search for a nice safe place to build her nest. She tried several different windows but she did not like any. They were either not safe or the area was too noisy or people living on the other side of wall did not want any bird making their home on their window. By the end of the day she was very tired and frustrated as she had found no safe place for her nest. She got tired and she sat on a window ledge and decided to call it a day. She was going to spend the night on this window and in the morning she will start her search again. At dawn, she noticed some activities inside the window. There was a man who was busy doing something. Suddenly she noticed the man opening the window, she became fearful and hid behind the big grey box. But soon she could not believe her good fortune. When the man moved away from the window, there was some fresh bread for her and just in time because she was hungry. Pigeon knew she had found the perfect place to build her nest and lay eggs. This was the home of the same couple who Myna was talking about. Pigeon was still hesitant but decided to take her chances.

She got busy with the nest building by finding the best twigs and leaves. In couple of days the nest was ready, a nice warm shelter in the safety of the widow ledge underneath the big box. Two days later she laid one egg in the evening after about ten hours she laid second egg. The

eggs would lie hustled to the mother pigeon for the whole day and father pigeon would sit with them in the evening through the night. The couple inside the house liked to stand by the window and watch the birds. Sometimes they will leave food for them. The pigeons were thankful for it so they did not have to go far for food. In about two weeks the eggs hatched and baby birds came out. But they still needed feeding and protection. Mom will bring food and feed the babies. Sometimes the babies will make noises and mother will notice that the nice couple will come running to the window to see what was wrong. The couple started feeding the babies and mother by leaving food for them every few hours.

The couple in the house were always curious to see the newborn and one day the woman was doing something and she thought she saw babies outside their hiding place. She was not sure so she tiptoed near the window to see what was all the commotion about. She nearly jumped with joy. She ran and got her husband and watched. It was a very beautiful scene. Babies were out with mother and they were trying to snatch food from mom's mouth. The couple stood there in silence with a smile on their face watching two beautiful white baby pigeons. The man wanted to give them food but the woman asked him to wait till the mother was gone and babies were back in their nest. After sometimes, the man ran quickly and put lots of food for all of them to feed on. The couple inside the home would watch with pride and joy the new babies. They will feed them every few hours and say goodnight to them in the night time. First thing in the morning, the man will feed them again and one more time before he went out. The woman will take over during the day time. The babies were getting stronger everyday. Sometimes they will peek inside the window or make lots of noise if there was no food. The mother pigeon would also make noise as if saying thank you for taking care of us by feeding us and keeping us safe.

One day the babies came out and tried to fly short distance. They were trying their wings. They did not go very far and stayed around their home. It was only matter of time when they would be able to fly away and be independent. One fine morning the couple woke up and they heard no sound. They went near the window and found that the pigeon family was quietly looking inside the window. They waited for their food very patiently and after their meal, all three of them made some pleasant sound as if saying thank you and good bye. They had one final look at the couple and flew away in the sky. The couple stood there watching them fly away. They were happy and sad at the same time. But they felt happy to be part of this family.

"When the nest becomes too small a bird is ready to spread its wings and fly." **Matshona Dhliwayo**

# A day in Park

The envelope maker stopped and listened quietly. There was noise coming from outside which was very unusual because the place was quiet this time of the day. Ben, the envelope maker was twenty five years old and had started this job very recently. He was enjoying the pace of work and support of his coworkers. His boss treated him well and he was quite happy with his wages too.

Ben was startled by the noise and he was very much bothered by that. He was wondering what was all the commotion about but was reluctant to take time off his work and did not want to go out to see what was happening. He looked at his watch and realized it was almost his lunch time. Usually he ate his lunch at the park bench and went for a short walk around the park to get some fresh air and exercise. He picked up his lunch and opened the door to check out the source of noise outside.

When he stepped out he was surprised to see what was going on. In the park across from the work place, a crowd of people had formed around a homeless man, who was sitting on the ground trying to get away from the angry crowd. Ben recognized him as he had encountered him few times around the corner street trying to move around in his wheelchair. He had exchanged polite pleasantries with him before. Some mornings, he picked up some breakfast and a drink for him. This homeless man had lost both his legs in war when he was in Army. They were both on first name basis and the man was called John.

John's wheelchair was nearby but he was not able to sit in the chair. On closer examination, Ben noticed a young girl had brought some food for him and a little boy, may be her brother,

was playing with a small puppy and also feeding him some bread. The crowd of people did not like the idea of a homeless person in such beautiful park and wanted him to go away some place else. The young girl looked very upset and she was pleading with the crowd that the homeless man was sitting there very peacefully and was not bothering anyone. Her little brother was also upset as he was witnessing such rude behavior by adults. He kept on playing with the puppy to keep him engaged while feeding him as well. Ben was devastated to witness such scene. He could not believe that they would treat such a decent handicap veteran so badly and disrespectfully who never bothered anyone and was always courteous. He lived on the street because he had no family, no job or stable home situation. He survived on a very small government pension that was never enough, but he was always polite and never asked for anything from anyone.

Ben could not stand it anymore and he crossed the street to meet the unruly crowd. He addressed them in a very polite manner and told them all about John. He said that it was not John's fault that he was in such situation but John was a gentleman. Initially Crowd did not want to listen to Ben but someone in the crowd told them to be quiet to listen to what Ben was saying. They looked around and saw the young girl and her brother treating John and his puppy with kindness and compession and Ben was also sharing his sandwich with John. Suddenly, they became very quiet and embarrassed of their own crass behavior. The crowd realized John was not doing any harm and was just enjoying a quiet day in the sunny park. They started apologizing to John as well the young girl. Someone from the crowd ran to the store next door and brought a cup of coffee for John. John was helped to his wheelchair by someone and made him comfortable. Everyone felt very ashamed of their uncivilized behaviour and could not recall how everything even started.

Slowly people apologized to John and started saying goodbye to him and leave. There were only few people left in the park, including the young girl, her brother and Ben. Brother and sister felt very happy that the situation was under control. They had witnessed something that they had never experienced in their life. They thanked Ben profusely for coming when he did and made everything right. John was also very thankful to Ben for helping him out. They broke out in roaring cheer in appreciation for Ben for what he just did.

Ben looked at his watch and realized that his lunch time was over and he needed to leave. Nevertheless he was very happy to know that he was able to save a helpless man from such disrespectful behaviour. He said goodbye to everyone and started crossing the street to go back to work. When he got to his work, he noticed his boss was standing there and smiling at him. He thanked him for his kind behaviour towards John. He had a small plate of hot lunch for Ben and told him to take few minutes to eat in the lunch room. Ben was truly thankful and took a bow and started for the lunchroom. He waited for the roar to subside, then he closed the door behind him.

Be kind, for every man is fighting a hard battle. ~ Plato

Printed in the United States
by Baker & Taylor Publisher Services